MW00973167
To Hope!
'Floral Frolic' 1st edition printing 1667 / 2000

Floral Frolic

By Cari Corene and
Amanda Coronado

Once upon a flower,
there were two fox friends.
Their names were Queenie
and Dawnsing.

"Let's pick flowers!"
Dawnsing said.

Queenie agreed, but
with one condition,
"I bet I can pick
better flowers!"

The two fox friends dashed in opposite directions.

"I'll pick flowers over here!"

"I'll pick flowers
over there!"

Queenie found
bee flowers.

Dawnsing found
butter flowers.

Queenie *almost* picked
BIG flowers.

Dawnsing picked
one little flower.

There were smelly flowers,
and sneezy flowers,

earthy flowers,
and breeeeeeeeezy flowers

Dawnsing frolicked
in pointy flowers!

Queenie pounced on puffy flowers!

Moon flowers
dotted meadows
like stars.

Noon flowers
stroked the blue
sunny sky.

When the friends found each other again on that same serene meadow, they'd had so much fun they nearly forgot their contest!

But they didn't quite forget. "My flowers are better," they each said at once.

"THESE FLOWERS ARE
PUUUURRRFECT!!

Dawnsing
nearly fell over!
Queenie really
puffed up!

Their friend Rawra had surprised them as she leapt out from the tall grass of the meadow. She was excited to see the vibrant array of flowers.

RWWRRR!

Rawra knew what needed to
be done to make them perfect!

Dawnsing couldn't find her flowers anymore. Queenie wasn't sure which flowers were hers either. The flowers had settled back to earth and made a perfect rainbow bouquet.

Extra Content

The Very First Floral Frolic Drawings!!

When I (Amanda) write, I tend to script and thumbnail simultaneously. The result is a pile of tiny drawings and unintelligable chicken scratch. When I thumbnail, I tend to try to get the idea out as fast as possible. Erasing is absolutely not allowed at this stage. If it's not working, I draw a new box and try again. The first three rows were composed and then I stopped to discuss ideas with Cari. The last row contains ideas for additional pages. Some of these were used, others completely scrapped. There was no point deciding at that moment; it's important to generate ideas and not throw them out right at the start.

Rough Drawing

“Flower Pile” Page Process

From the initial thumbnailing, we decided the book should open on the charcters and a pile of flowers. Cari immediately had an idea and went and sketched.

I took the rough drawing she did and enlarged it in Photoshop. I then went and did a pencil drawing on top of the enlarged roughs.

Some of the details on the charcters have changed a lot from this original drawing! Queenie, for instance, went from having a white tail, to a tail with red dashes on it! But mostly, I wasn’t really preplanning at this point; I was just having a lot of fun dawing the characters in a bed of flowers!

Finished Pencil Art

Did you know Cari painted Flower Pile **twice**??

Yes I did! Amanda and I really enjoy older childrens' books, which have a very rustic aesthetic. My first painting of Flower Pile mimicked old Golden books in color palette. We weren't happy with this look on o own work though. It wasn't representative of our styles, and we decided we wanted a more modern rainbc palette throughout the book. It did mean doing double the work for me, but actually sometimes I learn more from 'failures' than I do from first try successes. Flower Pile really set the tone for the rest of the pag in the book and I think it was worth the extra effort to paint it a second time. I don't excel at getting thing perfect on try number one, but I am pretty good at working hard at something until I get it right.

Cover Art
Drawing Progression

1 Concept

When we discussed what we wanted on the cover of the book, it was a given that it should be an image that is fun and playful. We also had our hearts set on a foil printing, so it was also a given that this was a thing I should plan for.

Foil printing can be fickle in nature, with the stamp sometimes shifting during printing. Because of this, I (Amanda) needed to plan for a cover that was in two parts- the underlying illustration and foil elements that would not look out of place if they were shifted slightly.

2 Thumbnail

I started off this drawing by making a quick thumbnail. The thumbnail is drawn in ink so I would have to commit to an idea. I used a gold pen to get a feel of were I would like the foil on the cover.

3 Enlarge In Photoshop

Next, I scanned the thumbnail and enlarged it in Photoshop. Here I made sure the front and back cover would lay out correctly.

I then converted the image to a single color, (I used light blue on this image,) and after that I printed an enlargement and I pencilled on top of it.

I usually do all my final drawings on 8.5 x 11 inch cardstock. This drawing was a little too large in dimensions for a regular cardstock sheet, so I taped two pieces togther. I then got to drawing!

As you can see, the logo has been dropped for this version. I finished the logo later in Illustrator and dropped the final illustration in after that. I left the butterflies in because I wanted to draw butterflies.

I really got into drawing foliage on the cover! After I had completed a large chunk, I realized I had drawn too much! It was much to busy, but at least I had Photoshop to help me clean it up.

5 Clean Up In Photoshop

The image is again scanned and edited in Photoshop. I removed and adjusted parts of the image I was unhappy with. I also refined my pencil lines.

Photoshop editing is great in that it allows for the flexibilty to make changes without destorying your original drawing.

6 Finishing

As I erased and cleaned up my lineart, I also added elements I forgot to draw and removed others that I didn't care for. In this drawing, I removed the foliage on the left side, which would be the back of the book. I did not leave enough room for text on the back, so the drawing definitely had to be adjusted. The extra plants were deleted and I added a spray of flowers across the top and bottom corner of the image.

After completion, I passed the drawing off to Cari. She made additional edits of her own. Then the drawing was enlarged again and reprinted on watercolor paper.

Cover Art
Painting Progression
1 Lineart Transfer.
2 Blendy first layer of paint.
Watercolor is all about knowing when to let the paint blend and flow and when to hold the paint ba and control it. When I (Cari) paint, I start by lightl printing finished pencils on watercolor paper anc then I go over the printout with a pencil.
After completing the lineart transfer, I soak the paper, staple it to a stretching board, and apply the first layer of paint. This means I'm painting wet paint on soaking wet paper. The paint is goin to blend everywhere, the goal is to create light bas colors rooted in environment lighting. When the soaked paper dries out (hours later) I begin painting loose details.
3 Start painting details.

4 Paint more details.

Watercolor paint is mostly transparent. This medium is all about glazing colors on top of each other. Let one layer of paint dry, paint on top of it, repeat. Here the base layer has established a gradient of colors from pink to blue. I then painted layers of detail on top of that blended layer. I painted with a somewhat wet brush on dry paper, so the paint was easier to control.

After I worked on the foliage I started on the foxes. I was concerned with getting the color palette well rounded between pink, blue, and a third color??? It turned out that third color was a goldish orange.

5 Start painting foxes.

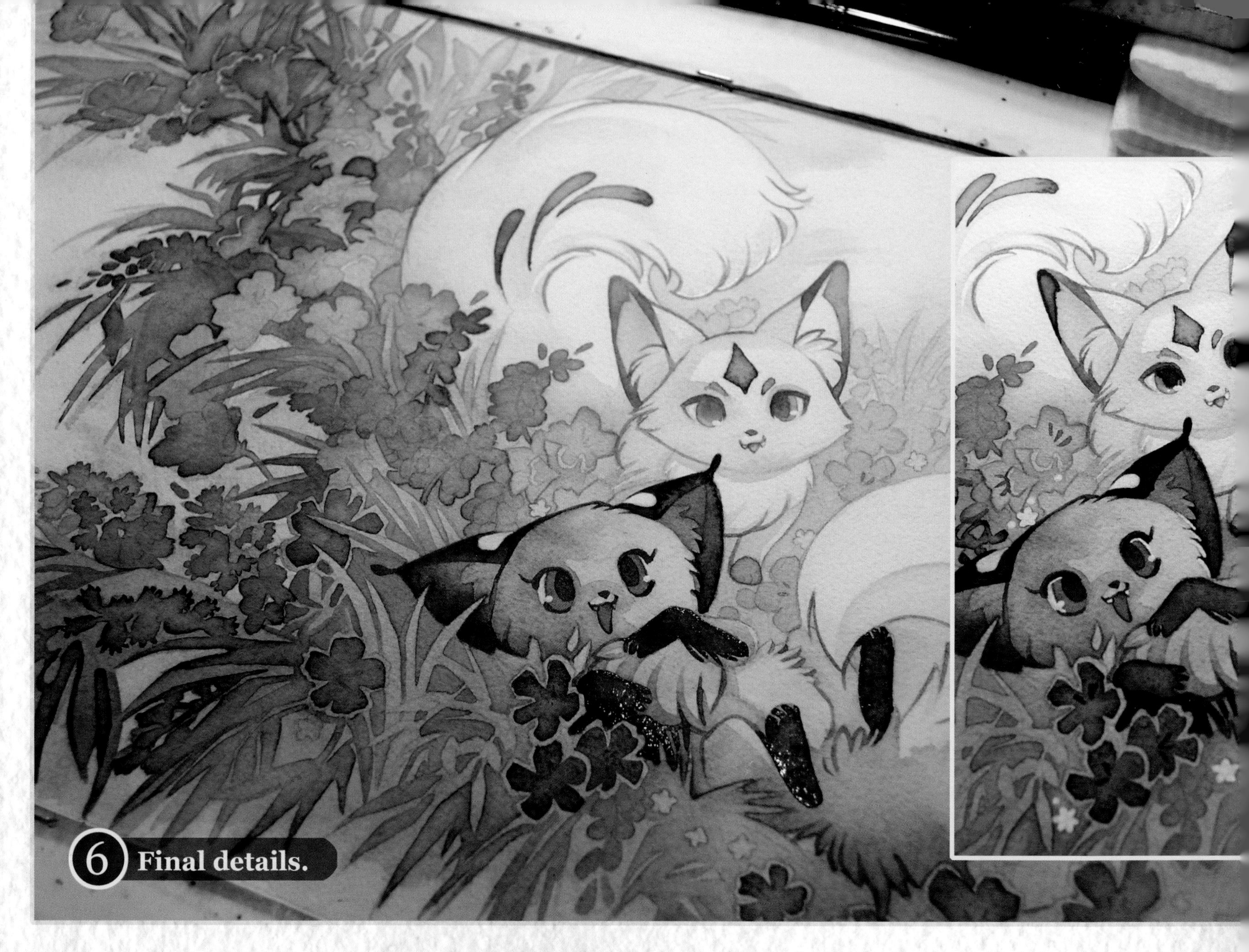

I know that the foxes are going to be the center of attention in this image so I want to visually represent that. Here I've made sure that the foxes are the highest contrast part of the image, both in light/dark value contrast as well as color hue contrast. I've painted dark browns on top of their light fur, giving them the darkest values in the image, and that orange and red will definitely stand out nicely against a cyan environment.

This image is a pretty good summary of how I paint most things. Start with broad, loose, blend colors. Gradually add layers of detail and layers color. It's also important to note that watercolo takes a lot of hard work practice! My first paintin were very bad, I ruined a lot of good drawings b trying to paint on them. But sometimes you lear more from failure than from getting it right on tl first try. Now go forth and paint!

The asthetic for Floral Frolic is painterly and lineless, but here are a few pieces we did of inked drawings with hard lined coloring! It's a completely different look! If the book had been done in this style, it would be a very different looking project.

Thank you so much for reading Floral Frolic!!

We really hope that you've enjoyed the book and this extra content section! We want to give a big thanl you here for everyone who supported Floral Frolic on Kickstarter!! It was you who funded the printing c this book and motivated us to complete the last half of the illustrations. This is our first children's book and it has been wonderful! Please know that putting this book out has been incredibly rewarding for us and we hope some fraction of our enjoyment can be felt here in your hands in the form of this book.

If you would like to follow our future projects, here is where we can be reached:

Amanda Coronado
devils-bakery.com
cinnamoron.deviantart.com

Cari Corene
caricorene.com
blix-it.deviantart.com

Floral Frolic, October 2015, first printing, printed in China.
Published by Cari Corene and Amanda Coronado.

Hardcover ISBN : 978-0-9966269-1-0

Contact information and more creative work may be found at:
devils-bakery.com and caricorene.com